THE HALLOWEEN HOUSE

by
ERICA SILVERMAN

Illustrations by
JON AGEE

FARRAR STRAUS GIROUX

SQUARE
FISH

To the Torn family,
especially Ralph, Adele, and Linda,
with love —E.S.

S Q U A R E
F I S H

An Imprint of Macmillan

Library of Congress Cataloging-in-Publication Data
Silverman, Erica.
 The Halloween house / Erica Silverman ; pictures by Jon Agee. — 1st ed.
   p. cm.
 Summary: The Halloween house, occupied by a variety of creatures, including werewolves, witches, bats, and skeletons,
turns out to be an unfortunate choice as a hideout for a couple of escaped convicts.
 [1. Halloween—Fiction. 2. Prisoners—Fiction. 3. Stories in rhyme. 4. Counting.] I. Agee, Jon, ill. II. Title.
PZ8.3.S58425Hal 1997
[E]—dc20   96-11593

ISBN-13: 978-0-312-38013-7 / ISBN-10: 0-312-38013-5

Originally published in the United States by Farrar, Straus and Giroux
Square Fish logo designed by Filomena Tuosto
First Square Fish Edition: August 2008
10 9 8 7 6 5 4 3 2 1
www.squarefishbooks.com

In the Halloween house,
in a dark, dingy den...

a papa werewolf crouched
with his little ones, *ten*.
"Howl," said the papa.
"We howl," said the ten.
So they howled through the night
in the dark, dingy den.

In the Halloween house,
on a bed made of pine,
a mama vampire woke
with her little ones, *nine*.
"Rise," said the mama.
"We rise," said the nine.
So they rose through the night
from the bed made of pine.

In the Halloween house,
on a slimy old plate,
a papa worm huddled
with his little ones, *eight*.
"Squirm," said the papa.
"We squirm," said the eight.
So they squirmed through the night
on the slimy old plate.

In the Halloween house,
under rafters near heaven,
a mama bat hung
with her little ones, *seven*.
"Swoop," said the mama.
"We swoop," said the seven.
So they swooped through the night
under rafters near heaven.

In the Halloween house,
above bent candlesticks,
a papa ghost hovered
with his little ones, *six*.
"Boooooo," said the papa.
"We booooooo," said the six.
So they boooooed through the night
above bent candlesticks.

In the Halloween house,
by a yawning fireside,
a mama monster played
with her little ones, *five*.
"Chase," said the mama.
"We chase," said the five.
So they chased through the night
by the yawning fireside.

In the Halloween house,
on a creaky cobwebbed floor,
a papa skeleton swayed
with his little ones, *four.*
"Dance," said the papa.
"We dance," said the four.
So they danced through the night
on the creaky cobwebbed floor.

In the Halloween house,
among junk and debris,
a mama spider wove
with her little ones, *three*.
"Swing," said the mama.
"We swing," said the three.
So they swung through the night
among junk and debris.

In the Halloween house,
where the books were askew,
a papa cat lurked
with his little ones, *two*.
"Pounce," said the papa.
"We pounce," said the two.
So they pounced through the night
where the books were askew.

In the Halloween house,
where the cauldron was hung,
a mama witch chanted
with her little witch, *one*.
"Fly," said the mama.
"I fly," said the one.
So she flew through the night
where the cauldron was hung.

In the Halloween house,
at the rise of the sun,
the parents all said hush
to their dear little ones.
"Vanish!" they whispered.

And then there were—none.

Halloween was over
at the rise of the sun.